MW01110315

BLACK JACK
LAST OF THE BIG ALLIGATORS

ROBERT M.
McCLUNG
illustrated by
Lloyd Sandford

Linnet Books • Hamden, Connecticut • 1991

Published 1991 as a Linnet Book,
an imprint of The Shoe String Press, Inc.
Hamden, Connecticut 06514

Library of Congress Cataloging-in-Publication Data

McClung, Robert M.
Black Jack : last of the big alligators /
Robert M. McClung ; illustrated by Lloyd Sandford.
p.   cm.
Summary: Black Jack the alligator is born, grows to maturity,
and escapes death at the hands of poachers.
1. Alligators—Juvenile fiction. [1. Alligators—Fiction.]
I. Sanford, Lloyd, ill. II. Title
PZ10.3.M115Bk   1991   91-14387   [Fic]—dc20
ISBN 0-208-02326-7

The paper in this book meets the minimum requirements
of American National Standard for Information Sciences—Permanence
of Paper for Printed Library Materials, ANSI Z39.48-1984 ⊗

Printed in the United States of America

The author wishes to thank the many individuals with the United States Fish and
Wildlife Service, and with the state game and fish commissions of Florida, Louisiana,
and Georgia, who provided him with information about alligators. The book *The
Alligator's Life History* by E. A. McIlhenny was very useful for detailed data unavailable
elsewhere. Special gratitude is due staff members of both Okefenokee and Savannah
National Wildlife Refuges, who enabled the author to observe alligators, their nests,
and eggs, in the wild; to Dr. Tully Pennington of Georgia Southern College, who was
very helpful concerning local flora and fauna; and to Dr. Herndon Dowling, Curator
of Reptiles at the New York Zoological Park, for his kindness in reading and criticizing
the manuscript.

CONTENTS

THE NEST

Old Min floated like a water-heavy log near the center of the pool. Only her eyes and nostrils showed, like knobby stubs of wood above the surface. The rest of the big alligator's body was hidden in the black depths. Old Min was watching and waiting—waiting for prey to come her way.

A cardinal flew over the pool, a flash of gleaming red in the June sunshine. A glittering blue dragonfly landed with a flutter of wings on a cypress knee. Old Min noticed these movements, but she did not stir. Her eyes were gray-green, each catlike pupil narrowed to a vertical slit in the strong sunlight. Old Min's eyesight was very keen. She saw everything about her.

Huge cypress trees rose from the water, their swollen bases covered with ferns, their branches hung with streamers of Spanish moss. A tangle of sweet bay and buttonbush rimmed the shores of the pool. Water lilies and pickerel weed crowded the shallows. An anhinga perched on a dead stub by the side of the pool and sunned itself, its silver-streaked wings spread wide. Mirror images

of all these surroundings were reflected in the dark clear waters of the great Okefenokee Swamp of southern Georgia.

As Old Min watched and waited, a snake crawled through the tall grass on the far shore and slithered into the water. It began to swim across the pool, its thick mottled body moving in lazy S curves. It was a poisonous cottonmouth, or water moccasin.

Old Min followed the snake for a moment with her eyes. Then she sank, with scarcely a ripple, and swam underwater to meet it. Coming up from below, she lunged forward and seized it with a quick sideways sweep of her huge, tooth-lined jaws.

Surfacing, she shook her head violently from side to side, preventing the writhing cottonmouth from striking at her eyes. The snake was good food, but its venom could poison her if it got into her bloodstream. Old Min champed down with her teeth, crushing the life out of her victim. In a moment the struggle was all over. She swallowed the snake in two or three greedy bites.

Flicking her tail lazily, the big alligator headed for shore. She stroked with her tail, her legs trailing close to her body. When she was submerged, transparent membranes slid back across her eyes, protecting them from the water. Muscular valves closed her nostrils, and hinged flaps of skin shut the creased ear openings behind her eyes.

When she reached the small island that bordered one edge of the pool, Old Min crawled out on the bank and basked in the warm sunshine. Stretched out full length, she measured a little more than eight feet in length. She weighed about 175 pounds. Male alligators sometimes grow much larger, but she was good-sized for a female.

Old Min's sides, legs, and underparts were covered with row upon row of smooth horny scales. Her head and back, however, were heavily armored with big bony plates. Most of these plates had raised keels, forming numerous jagged ridges down her back and tail.

Her belly scales were pale yellowish, but the rest of Old Min's body was chiefly a dark sooty gray. Each of her front feet had five toes, each of her hind feet four. The three inner toes on each foot were armed with claws.

After soaking up the sunshine for half an hour, Old Min stirred. Rising on her squat legs, she scrambled up the bank and along a path that her heavy body had cleared through the reeds and tall grass. A passing kingfisher rattled in alarm, but Old Min paid no attention to it.

A few feet inland she came to a small clearing with a black gum tree near its center. Under the tree was a big mound of dried leaves and grass. It was Old Min's nest, built several years before. Alligators often use the same nest year after year. Each spring they repair the mound and add new material to it. Old Min had mated several weeks before.

Now she was going to get the nest ready for a new clutch of eggs.

Near the edge of the clearing, Old Min seized a clump of grass in her jaws and pulled it out by the roots. Backing over the mound, she dropped the grass on top of it. Then she crawled forward over the new material and packed it in before going for another mouthful. She worked steadily for several hours. By dusk the mound was more than three feet high and nearly seven feet across at the base. After dark she returned to the pool.

The next morning Old Min started work soon after sunrise. Pivoting on the top of the mound, she scooped out a big hole with her hind feet. This hole she filled, after repeated trips, with dripping mouthfuls of leaves and muck that she gathered in the shallow water. When all the wet material was packed in, she once again hollowed out a cavity in the rounded top. The nest was ready.

Straddling the cavity with her hind legs, Old Min began to lay her eggs. She paused only briefly to rest, and in half an hour she was finished. She had laid twenty-nine eggs in all. Alligators sometimes lay as few as a dozen eggs, sometimes sixty or more.

Each egg was nearly three inches long. It looked quite a bit like a big chicken egg, except that both ends were equally rounded. The white shell was hard and brittle.

Old Min covered the stacked eggs with a foot or more of wet leaves and muck. Then she crawled back and forth over the nest, packing in the material and smoothing it over. Finished at last, she crawled into the sluggish stream that flowed along one side of her pool and began to hunt for something to eat. Her activities had made her hungry.

The nest was only a few feet from Old Min's pool and from the den that she had dug in the bank as a retreat. For the next few weeks she stayed close to the nest most of the time. She was keeping an eye on it, guarding her eggs against possible danger. One night a turtle crawled up on the big mound and laid its eggs in the nest too. They did no harm to the alligator eggs.

A raccoon dug into the mound several nights afterward. It found many of the turtle eggs and ate them. The masked robber did not have time to dig deeper and uncover the alligator eggs, however. Old Min discovered him on the nest. Hissing with anger, she came charging up the path, and the raccoon beat a hasty retreat.

One afternoon, two weeks later, the old alligator saw a canoe coming downstream with two boys in it. They spotted the mounded nest a few feet inland and headed for shore to investigate it. Old Min raised her head out of the water. Puffing up with air, she hissed at the boys, her jaws gaping. Then she swam

toward them. The boys did not wait to see
whether Old Min was bluffing or not. They
scrambled into their canoe and paddled away
as fast as they could go.

Week after week went by with the hot summer sun beating down on the heap of decay-
ing vegetation. Frequent rains kept the nest
material damp most of the time. The buried
eggs needed both heat and humidity in order
to develop properly.

The temperature inside the nest averaged five or six degrees higher than the temperature outside. It also did not vary as much as the outside temperature did. Deep in the dark, warm incubator, each little alligator grew and developed inside its shell.

The tiny alligator lay curled up, its back pressed to the shell, its tail tucked between its hind legs. Oxygen passed through the porous shell, and the growing embryo received this life-giving gas through blood vessels in the membranes that surrounded it. It received nourishment from the egg yolk, to which it was connected by a cord.

The first egg hatched in early September, sixty-three days after Old Min had laid it. The little alligator pushed against one end of the egg with a hard knob, or caruncle, at the tip of his upper jaw. The shell cracked under the pressure, and the baby reptile pushed its head out. It uttered several soft grunts, "Umph, umph, umph!" Soon the calls of other hatchlings sounded around it.

Old Min heard the grunts of her young ones. Climbing out of her pool, she crawled over to the nest and bit off some of the debris from the top of the mound. She was making it easier for the babies to emerge.

First one little alligator pushed his way through the matted vegetation, then another. Soon half a dozen were on top of the nest. All had scrambled up through the same hole. They grunted at each other, and their mother grunted back at them. One after another the young ones clambered down the sides of the mound and followed Old Min as she crawled back toward the water. Without even hesitating, they slithered into the pool behind her. Before the day was over, all twenty-nine youngsters were hatched and in the water.

The baby gators were about eight inches long. They were much darker than Old Min —almost black—and had bright yellow stripes on their sides. One of them had fewer stripes than the others, and most of his scales were a shiny blue-black. This one would be known as Black Jack.

THE POOL AND THE DEN

Each young alligator had a swollen belly for several days, a remnant of the yolk sac that had nourished it all through its development in the egg. These swellings soon disappeared, and the youngsters began to hunt food for themselves. They snapped down wriggling tadpoles and minnows. They stalked little crayfish in the shallows and pursued tiny frogs and toads. Most of their food, however, consisted of insects.

Black Jack swam after water beetles and dragonfly nymphs, snapping them down. He came up under moths or flies or grasshoppers that had fallen into the water and devoured them with a gulp. Anything that he could swallow was fair game.

Sometimes Old Min caught a snake or large fish for her dinner. Then Black Jack and his brothers and sisters gathered around the old alligator and fed on the scraps of flesh that floated away from her jaws.

The little alligators ranged all over Old Min's pool, which she kept free of vegetation except at the edges. Sometimes they explored the stream that flowed by the pool, or ventured into the nearby swampy meadows in search of food. Old Min did not seem to pay any attention to them. But she was usually close by to defend them if any danger threatened. Given half a chance, many animals that lived in the big swamp would make a meal of baby alligators.

A great horned owl seized a youngster as
it was clambering ashore one evening. Grasp-
ing the wriggling little gator in its talons, the
owl flew off.

That same night a big raccoon caught another one in shallow water. The baby alligator grunted in alarm, and Old Min came
rushing to the rescue as fast as she could. But
she was too late. The raccoon carried its victim ashore and into a tangle of underbrush.

Several days later a three-foot-long garfish ate two of the young alligators before Old Min caught the huge fish and ate it in turn. The following week a six-foot bull alligator invaded the pool while Old Min was hunting in the swamp. He killed another. When Old Min returned, she drove him off.

Black Jack had several narrow escapes. One day a giant snapping turtle almost got him, but he wriggled away just in time. Another

day he was dozing on a log when a big white
bird, an American egret, spied him. Stalking
toward him through the shallow water, the
egret stabbed downward with a lightning
stroke of its long, sharp bill and seized him.
Black Jack squealed with pain, and Old Min

thrashed across the pond and lunged at the egret. Dropping Black Jack, the egret gave a frightened squawk and took off.

By early November only sixteen of the original twenty-nine young alligators were left. They had grown quite a bit during the past two months. Black Jack measured fifteen inches, twice as long as when he had hatched.

The weather had become much cooler. During the autumn the leaves of many swamp trees had briefly flamed red or orange or yellow, then dropped and floated on the black waters. Reeds and other swamp growth were yellowing. As the temperatures of both air and water fell, Old Min and the young alligators lost much of their interest in eating. Day by day they became more sluggish.

Alligators, like all reptiles, are cold-blooded animals. They cannot maintain a constant body temperature independently of their surroundings, as warm-blooded mammals and

birds can. Alligators must gain their body
heat from outside sources—the warmth of the
sun, the air, and the water. When they are
cold, they seek a warmer spot. If they get
too hot, they move to a cooler area.

Thus, alligators are most active in summer,
when both the air and water are warm. As
winter approaches the outside sources of heat
dwindle. Both air and water become cooler,
and the alligator's body temperature drops.
Then alligators become very sluggish. They
do not eat or move about very much.

By late December the waters of the swamp

were much colder than they had been in the summer. The air temperature sometimes fell close to the freezing point at night. Winter had arrived. Old Min and the little alligators retired into their den.

The den was a long tunnel, or cave, which Old Min had dug in the side of her pool. From its underwater entrance, it extended nearly fifteen feet under the bank. It widened at the rear, forming an underground pool with a pocket of air above it.

Old Min and her young ones stayed in the den practically all winter long. For many days at a time they scarcely moved, for their bodily functions had slowed down to almost nothing. They were hibernating, waiting for the warmth of springtime to waken them again.

Once in a while, if the day was unusually mild for winter, Black Jack or one of his brothers would venture briefly out of the den and bask in the pale sunshine. But most of the time they remained hidden and quiet, like their mother.

The coldest months—January and February—passed. In March the air became noticeably warmer, the days longer and sunnier. At the same time the alligators began to stir about more frequently. The water was starting to warm up, and new vegetation sprouted along the edges of the pool. After their long period of inactivity, Old Min and the young ones took up their active life again.

Golden trumpet flowers bloomed here and there throughout the swamp, and countless bright yellow spikes of "never-wet" lilies nodded above the dark waters. Big yellow and brown swallowtails fluttered through the April sunshine, and mockingbirds sang from high branches.

At night the great swamp resounded with the springtime chorus of frogs and toads, the rolling thunder of bull alligators bellowing for mates. Old Min responded to the call one May night and mated once more. Several weeks later she began to get her nest ready for a new clutch of eggs.

During the summer many of the yearling alligators left the pool and struck off on their own. But Black Jack and five of his brothers

and sisters remained. By early fall they each measured a little over two feet in length. Most alligators grow at the rate of a foot or so a year until they are seven or eight years old. From then on they grow more slowly.

One evening, in the last week in August, Black Jack swam out into the stream to hunt for something to eat. Fireflies glowed above him in the thickening dusk, and a red bat flicked over the pond lilies after insects. Faint in the distance Black Jack heard the scream of a bobcat, then the quavering call of a barred owl.

The moon began to rise, pale and ghostly over the treetops. Black Jack snapped down several small garfish and then an unwary young water rat that swam almost into his jaws. Belly full, he floated lazily on the surface. Two of his brothers were nearby, and Old Min was cruising back and forth fifty feet downstream.

Suddenly, around a bend, a bright beam
of light appeared, playing back and forth
across the water. After a moment it settled
on Black Jack. His eyes, reflecting the light
back, glowed orange-yellow in the darkness.
The strange light came from a kind of lantern called a bull's-eye lamp. It was held by
a man sitting in the bow of a flat-bottomed
boat. Behind him sat another man, who was
poling the boat through the thick growth of

water weeds. These men were alligator hunters. They killed alligators for their hide, which made very fine leather. The men could get a good price for every hide they took.

Huge and black, the boat drifted slowly toward Black Jack. The glare of the light dazzled him, and he lay motionless on the surface, as if hypnotized. Soon the boat was less than a dozen feet away. The man with the light picked up a hand ax and waited.

Finally within reach, he brought down the sharp blade in a murderous blow aimed at Black Jack's head. At that same instant the boat hit a snag, and the sudden jolt threw the hunter off balance. Black Jack felt a rush of air and water as the blade struck the surface close to his head. Startled, he sank to the bottom and swam to the nearby den.

The hunters, however, were not finished. In a moment their lantern picked up the twin orange reflections from the much larger eyes of Old Min. Holding their light steady on this new target, they drifted closer and closer to her. She too seemed hypnotized by the glare. When the man with the ax was close enough, he struck again with all his strength.

The crushing blow hit the big alligator between the eyes, splitting her skull. For a moment she thrashed wildly, then lay still. She was dead.

The hunters pulled her body alongside with a hooked pole and dragged it into the boat beside the bodies of three smaller alligators that they had already killed. Before they left the area that night they killed two of Black Jack's brothers as well.

GROWING PAINS

Old Min was gone, but Black Jack stayed on in the familiar pool, retiring to the old den each winter. By late summer of his fourth year he measured more than five feet in length and weighed nearly thirty pounds. He was big enough to tackle most prey that came his way.

Sometimes Black Jack lay half-hidden on the bank and waited for his dinner to come to him. If an unwary bird—or perhaps a raccoon or opossum—came close enough, he would lash out with his tail and sweep the victim toward his waiting jaws.

Sometimes, if the bird or mammal was swimming, Black Jack submerged and stalked his prey underwater. Then he came up from the depths and seized it. If the animal struggled, he pulled it under and drowned it. When the prey was too big to swallow all at once, he rolled with it in the water until he had twisted off a portion that he could manage in a gulp.

Much of his food was fish—catfish, gar, bass, bowfin, and others. He ate turtles, too, after crushing the shell with his powerful jaws. When Black Jack sank below the surface to hunt, flaps of skin at the back of his mouth closed, sealing off the mouth cavity from the throat and air passages behind. In this way he was able to open his jaws without getting water into his lungs.

His broad muzzle was armed with eighty sharp conical teeth—forty in the upper jaw and forty in the lower. As Black Jack grew and his jaws increased in size, the caps of his first small teeth fell off and were replaced by larger teeth beneath them pushing into position. His teeth would be replaced a number of times in this manner as he grew up.

One day Black Jack had an unpleasant surprise when he snapped at a dead fish floating on the surface. As soon as he seized it, he felt a sharp pressure in the roof of his mouth. A huge metal hook was lodged in his upper jaw. It had been hidden in the dead fish by alligator hunters. The hook was attached to a length of wire at the end of a strong line tied to a tree trunk on the nearby shore. He was caught.

Black Jack shook his head violently from side to side as he pulled and twisted against the hook. The water foamed while he rolled and thrashed, struggling to get away. Finally the hook tore through the flesh of his mouth, and he broke free. If he had swallowed it he never would have escaped.

Black Jack had other dangerous encounters during his growing-up years. He saw boats and men a number of times. The men were usually fishermen and did him no harm. But

once a man in a boat hit him a sharp blow
with a paddle as he floated on the surface,
almost breaking his back. The next year a
boatman shot at him as he lay sunning himself on the bank. The bullet creased the plates

on the back of his neck and sent him scrambling quickly into the water and away.

Several times at night he saw mysterious lights shining across the black waters, as when Old Min had been killed. Experience gradually taught him to submerge and hide at the mere sight of lights or boats or men.

By the spring of his fifth year, Black Jack measured six feet in length and weighed perhaps forty pounds. This size was just a small fraction of what he might attain if he lived his full natural life.

One evening, in mid-April, a big female alligator invaded Black Jack's pool, followed

closely by a nine-foot-long bull. The mating season had arrived, and the big bull was in no mood to allow a younger male near him. He whacked the water threateningly, then lunged at Black Jack with open jaws. Black Jack retreated quickly, since he was no match for the much bigger bull. Instead, he sought refuge in the nearby swamp.

Even there the newcomer would not leave him alone. For several days he pursued Black Jack whenever he saw him. The big bull was claiming the pool and surrounding marsh as his own. He finally forced Black Jack to quit the old familiar territory entirely.

For most of one day Black Jack cruised through a shimmering expanse of open swamp —called a prairie in the Okefenokee—following narrow runs already cleared by alligators among the water lilies and other aquatic plants. Now and then a startled wood duck or snowy egret took off with a frightened squawk ahead of him. Forests of cypress loomed in the distance, and on either side of him were many small tree-covered islands.

Near dusk he came to a cleared pool beside one of the islands. As he hunted for food, a big female alligator came toward him with open jaws. She had a nearby nest and was defending her territory. Once again Black Jack retreated.

After crossing another expanse of swamp, he came to a second island. There, close to shore, the run that he had been following widened into a small pond. Black Jack caught several fish and ate them. He remained in the pool that night and all the next day. There was plenty of food around, and no big alligators to bother him. He stayed on and on. This place would be his new home.

Black Jack widened the pool during the summer, tearing out lilies and other vegetation until he had cleared an area almost twenty feet across. He deepened the pool too, digging at the bottom with his claws, then sweeping the mud away with his tail. He was making his own "gator hole."

As fall approached, he began to work on a den as well. Tearing away roots with his teeth, he dug into the bank. He pushed dirt out of the underwater entrance of the lengthening tunnel with his hind feet, then spread the silt with sweeps of his tail. By late fall the den extended nearly ten feet under the bank. His winter retreat was ready.

By the spring of his eighth year Black Jack measured nearly 8 feet in length and weighed about 150 pounds. During the past two years he had matured. For the first time he was ready to mate. He was able to roar for the first time, too.

Puffing up with air, Black Jack raised his head in the water and forced the air out in a series of powerful coughs that vibrated across the swamp like the sounds of a mighty drum. The water boiled around him as his body contracted again and again with the sudden jerks that forced the sounds from his throat. At the same time, glands opened on either side of his chin, spreading a strong musky scent through the warm spring air. Both the sounds and the scent served as signals to female alligators and as warnings to rival bulls.

One evening Black Jack left his pool and wandered through the surrounding swamp in search of a mate. He roared repeatedly and heard answering roars from other bulls out roaming for the same reason. The bellows of one bull began to sound closer and closer. Soon a female alligator came into sight, closely followed by a bull about the same size as Black Jack.

For a moment the two males stared balefully at one another. Each whacked his tail angrily from side to side and hissed a similar warning. Then they both rushed to the attack.

With open jaws the other bull lunged for Black Jack's foreleg. But before the tooth-lined trap could snap shut, Black Jack seized the rival's lower jaw in his own teeth and held on with a bulldog grip.

Their muzzles locked together, the two bulls rolled over and over in the water, legs and tails thrashing. Black Jack felt the other's claws raking his belly. He bellowed with rage, and his opponent broke free. Turning swiftly,

Black Jack attacked again and slashed his rival's leg with his sharp teeth. The other bull backed off, hissing loudly. He wanted no more of the fight.

Black Jack pursued the other for a moment, then turned back to the female. He roared as he came toward her, and she answered with a soft rattle that sounded like *snar-r-r-r*. Battered but victorious, Black Jack swam over beside her. Soon they mated in the water.

BIGGEST GATOR OF THEM ALL

Year after year passed, and Black Jack continued to live in the pool he had made when he was five years old. Every summer he deepened it and widened it. Nearly every fall he dug his den farther into the bank.

When he was ten years old, he measured nearly ten feet in length and weighed over three hundred pounds. During the next year he added another six inches and another fifty pounds. From then on, he grew more slowly. By the time he was thirty years old he measured a few inches more than fifteen feet and weighed nearly six hundred pounds. He was the biggest alligator in the Okefenokee.

In bygone days alligators sometimes reached sixteen, seventeen, or even eighteen feet in length. The known record is nineteen feet and two inches. But in recent years very few alligators have survived long enough to approach

that size. Left alone, an alligator might live
for sixty or seventy years—perhaps quite a
bit longer.

By this time Black Jack claimed as his own
domain most of the territory for a mile or so
in every direction from his pool. Every springtime he ranged far and wide, looking for
mates and chasing off smaller bulls. On spring
evenings his roars sounded like thunder rolling over the swamp. "I'll bet that's Black
Jack!" the people who heard him said. The

giant alligator was well-known throughout the region. His huge size and dark color made him easy to recognize.

There were not nearly so many alligators in the Okefenokee these days as there had been when Black Jack was a youngster. Thousands had been killed by alligator hunters during the intervening years. Throughout the entire range of the alligator—from the Carolina Low Country to the Florida Everglades and the bayous of Louisiana and eastern Texas—the number was decreasing. In many parts of the South, alligators had vanished altogether.

Black Jack continued to have his share of narrow escapes. He was shot at several times. On summer evenings he continued to see the night lights of alligator hunters now and again. Ever more cautious and experienced, he sank at first sight of them and hid away. Through the years man had been his principal enemy.

A time came, however, when an even greater danger threatened. The great Okefenokee Swamp began to dry out. For a whole year there had been very little rainfall, and water levels gradually dropped throughout the swamp. There was even less rainfall the year afterward, and a third summer came with no sign of relief.

Day after day the summer sun blazed down, drying up the shimmering wet prairies and exposing the black peat bottom that in normal years was covered with four or five feet of water. Streams and gator runs became shallow trickles, then mudholes. Water vanished

nearly everywhere except in the deepest holes.

Black Jack's pool became smaller and smaller as the precious water evaporated. He had dug deep, however, and in July it still held four feet of water at its deepest point. Alligator holes such as his were the only pockets of water left throughout much of the swamp.

Fish and frogs and turtles gathered there in great numbers, and water birds crowded the banks. Every evening deer and other mammals of the swamp came to the pool to drink. Black Jack's home saved the life of many kinds of wildlife during the great drought.

As the peat bottom of the swamp dried out, fires began to break out in the Okefenokee. Flames swept across the once watery prairies and killed much of the remaining wildlife. A number of animals trying to escape the flames took refuge in Black Jack's pool.

Black Jack stayed in his den much of the time that summer. He was protected there from the searing heat of the sun and the scorching fires that burned around him. Whenever he was hungry, the wildlife gathered around his pool provided him with plenty of food. He usually fed on the weakened or sick animals, for they were easiest to catch. Often he ate animals that were already dead.

In the autumn life-giving rains came at last. The smoldering fires gradually burned out, and the prairies slowly refilled with water. Once again the remaining wildlife spread out over the vast swamp. Gator holes had helped many animals to survive.

Several years after the great drought Okefenokee Swamp was made a national wildlife
refuge under the control of the United States
Fish and Wildlife Service. Some years later
a levee or sill was built along one edge of the
swamp to help keep water levels up in times
of little rainfall.

All the wildlife within the swamp was protected by law. But poachers continued to hunt
alligators in defiance of any regulations. They
were seldom caught, in spite of all the efforts
of the refuge staff. The swamp was just too
big—close to forty miles long and twenty-five
miles wide. There were too many places in
this huge watery wilderness where the poachers
could hunt without being discovered.

Near dusk one summer evening a flat-bottomed boat with two men in it slid silently through the swamp and approached Black Jack's den. The skins of four small alligators that the men had already killed that day lay in the bottom of the boat.

Black Jack saw the approaching boat and took refuge in his den. The hunters had seen Black Jack too. Coming right into his pool, they discovered the underwater entrance to his lair. The man in the bow of the boat probed into the hole with a long hooked pole. He was trying to force Black Jack to come out. Black Jack felt the sharp hook scraping against his back. Irritated, he turned his head and broke the pole in two with one snap of his mighty jaws.

Then the hunters tried something different. Bringing the boat to the edge of the pool, the man in the bow climbed ashore carrying a shotgun. He poked about and found a small airhole between a tangled mass of roots. It led down to Black Jack's den, several feet below. The poacher aimed his gun into the hole and pulled the trigger.

Lying directly beneath the opening, Black Jack felt the sudden sharp sting of the pellets in his side. He hissed angrily and swept out of the den, coming up beside the boat just as the man with the gun was getting back in.

Shouting with excitement, the poacher raised his gun to shoot once again. At the same time Black Jack submerged and swam under the boat. He boiled up on the other side and struck the bow of the boat a shattering blow with his huge tail. There was a sharp sound of splintering wood, and the boat rocked so violently that the two hunters—both standing—fell into the water. The gun sailed through the air and landed in the mud.

The two hunters, sputtering with fear and excitement, floundered toward land as fast as they could go. They knew that alligators very seldom attacked people and that there were

no authentic records of them ever killing any-
one. But that information was cold comfort
when they were in the water next to an
angry gator like Black Jack.

Black Jack circled in the center of the pool
for a moment, watching as his two enemies
splashed toward shore. Then he hissed angrily
and surged after them. His great jaws snapped
shut just a few inches from the foot of the
second man as he was scrambling desperately
up the bank.

The two poachers didn't waste any time.
Plunging into the underbrush, they headed
for the other side of the island as fast as they
could go.

They did not find safety there, however.
One of the refuge staff—a game protector—
was in a boat on the other side of the island.
He heard the shot, then saw the two hunters
as they came out of the undergrowth a few
minutes later.

After hauling the two men into his boat, the game protector circled around the island to Black Jack's pool. He saw the splintered boat with the four alligator hides in it. He saw the shotgun lying in the mud. All of this evidence would help to convict the poachers when they were tried for illegal hunting.

The game protector knew that the pool was Black Jack's, but he saw no sign of the big alligator. He was worried, for he did not trust the story the two hunters had told him. There was nothing he could do about Black Jack now, however. After gathering up the gun and the alligator skins, he headed back to headquarters. There he would turn his prisoners and evidence over to the sheriff.

Early the next morning he went back to the pool, hoping that he might see Black Jack. When he arrived, the big alligator was lying on the bank in plain view, sunning himself. Black Jack raised his huge head and hissed, his fierce eyes glowing in the bright sunlight. Then he slid into the water and disappeared.

"All right, Black Jack," the game protector said. "I just wanted to make sure that you were O.K." He turned and headed away.

An hour later Black Jack floated on the surface of his pool and looked about with his catlike eyes. A shimmering green dragonfly fluttered past his jaws and landed on a cypress knee. Black Jack didn't pay any attention to it. He closed his eyes and dozed.

AFTERWORD

"The alligators were in such incredible numbers, and so close together from shore to shore, that it would have been easy to have walked across on their heads, had the animals been harmless." Thus the naturalist William Bartram described a scene on a Florida river nearly 200 years ago.

During the next century and a half, however, alligators were increasingly exploited for their hides. Many millions were killed, a large proportion of them before they reached breeding size, to satisfy the demand for alligator suitcases, bags, and other leather goods. During the first half of the twentieth century, the population in many areas dropped to the vanishing point.

Because of this alarming decline, Florida outlawed all alligator hunting within the state in the early 1950s. Many other states with surviving populations followed suit. In 1967 the federal government declared the alligator an endangered species, legally protected everywhere.

Poachers, however, continued to hunt the alligator in defiance of regulations. The demand for alligator leather was greater than ever, and the rewards of illegal hunting were high compared to the risk. Poaching was big business: hunters often operated in organized groups, equipped with high-speed airboats, searchlights, and two-way radios to warn each other of approaching game wardens. The slaughter of alligators continued.

In response, federal and state game protectors stepped up their efforts against poachers, tracking them down relentlessly and exacting stiff penalties for their outlaw activities. The illegal hunting was finally brought under control, and alligator numbers began to increase nearly everywhere. By the 1990s, populations had recovered completely and the alligator was no longer endangered. Several states once again have permitted limited and strictly-regulated alligator hunts.

America's largest reptile, the alligator is a picturesque and highly interesting part of the natural scene in many Southern states. It must be safeguarded for this and future generations to see and enjoy in its natural habitat.